W9-BLG-547

SAMMY SPIDER'S FIRST SHAVUOT

Sylvia A. Rouss

illustrated by
Katherine Janus Kahn

KAR-BEN
PUBLISHING

KAR-BEN PUBLISHING, INC.
A division of Lerner Publishing Group
241 First Avenue North
Minneapolis, MN 55401 U.S.A.
1-800-4-Karben

Website address: www.karben.com

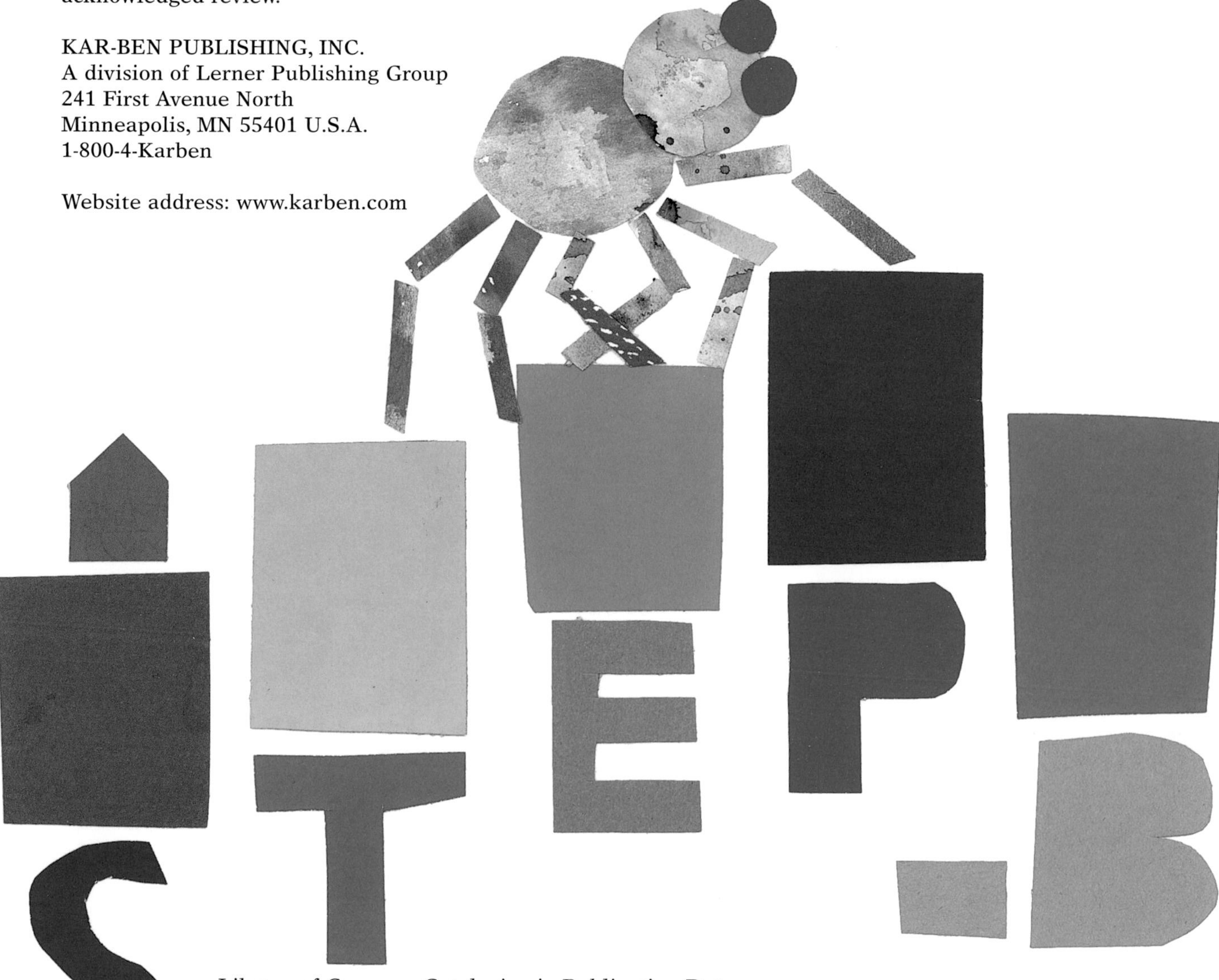

Library of Congress Cataloging-in-Publication Data

Rouss, Sylvia A.
Sammy Spider's first Shavuot / by Sylvia A. Rouss ; illustrated by Katherine Janus Kahn.
p. cm.
Summary: Sammy Spider lowers himself down on a strand of webbing to get a closer look at the Shapiro family's preparations for Shavuot, a holiday celebrating the time when God gave the Torah to Moses. Includes a recipe for making blintzes.
ISBN: 978-0-8225-7224-4 (lib. bdg. : alk. paper)
[1. Shavuot—Fiction. 2. Spiders—Fiction.] I. Kahn, Katherine, ill. II. Title.
PZ7.R7622Saq 2008
[E]—dc22 2006039739

Manufactured in the United States of America
1 2 3 4 5 6 - JR - 12 11 10 09 08 07

To Hayden Sara, my newest source of inspiration.
—S.A.R.

In loving memory of Ichil and Shendl Wugshul, and their daughters Lisa and Giena, who perished in the Holocaust. And to Eva who survived.
—K.J.K.

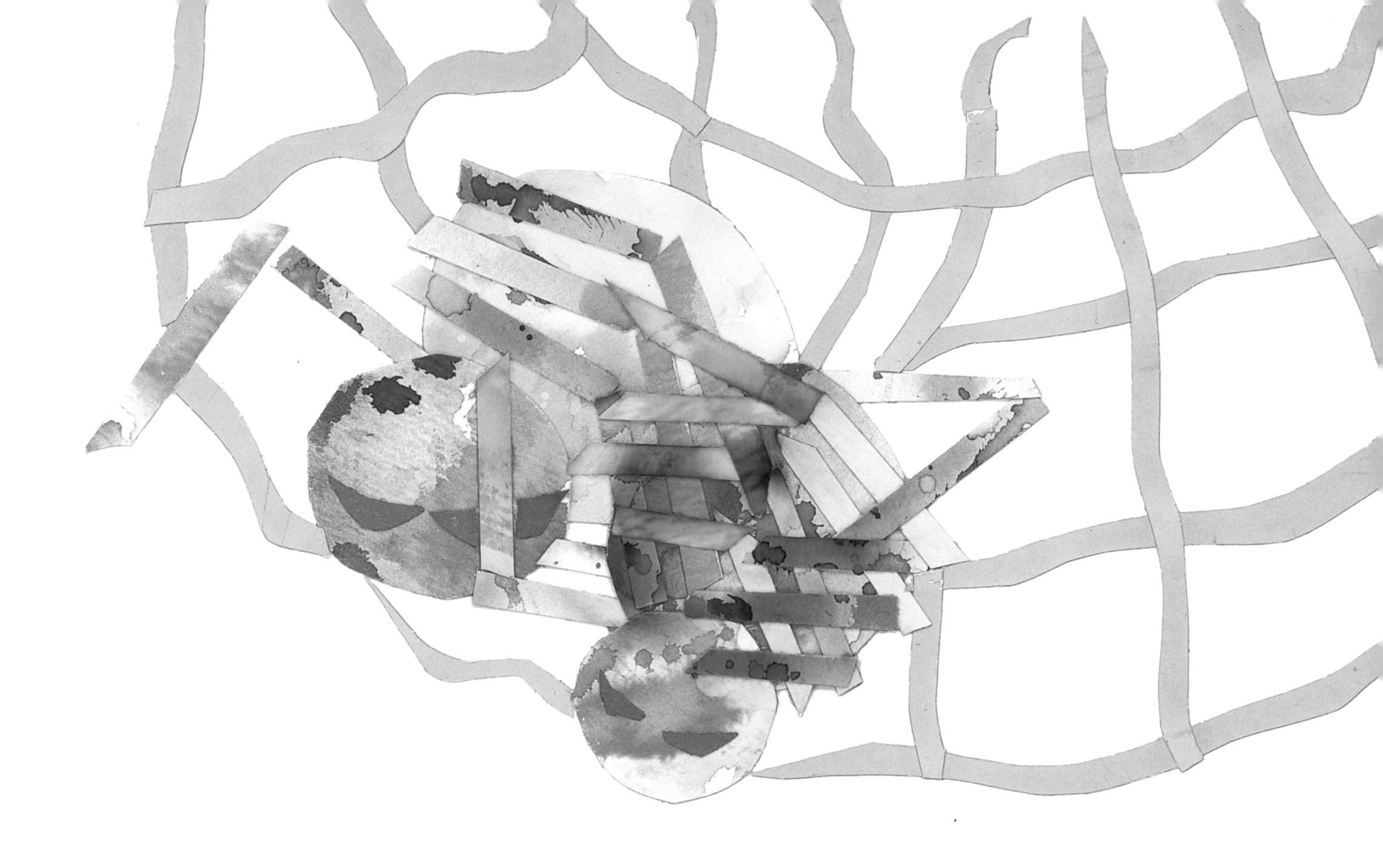

On a warm afternoon near the end of spring, Sammy Spider and his mother were snuggled in their web on the Shapiros' kitchen ceiling.

Sammy glanced down and noticed Mrs. Shapiro carefully measuring a cupful of flour.

"What is Mrs. Shapiro doing?" Sammy asked.

"She is following a recipe for making blintzes.

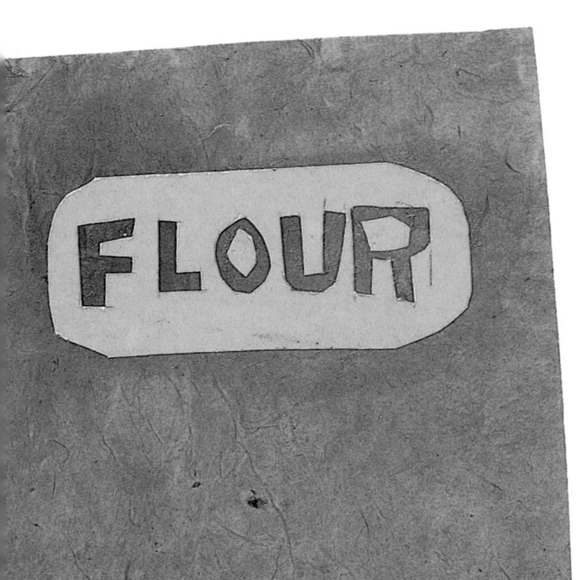

Mrs. Shapiro's Blintz Recipe

Pancakes

1 cup flour

2 eggs

1½ cup milk

1. *Mix the flour, eggs, and milk together. Pour a small amount of oil in a frying pan and heat.*
2. *Drop a spoonful of batter into the pan, tilting it to coat the pan.*
3. *When the blintz is lightly browned, remove it from the pan.*

“She will serve them this evening when the holiday of Shavuot begins.”

“What’s a recipe?” Sammy asked.

“It’s a list of instructions,” Mrs. Spider answered.

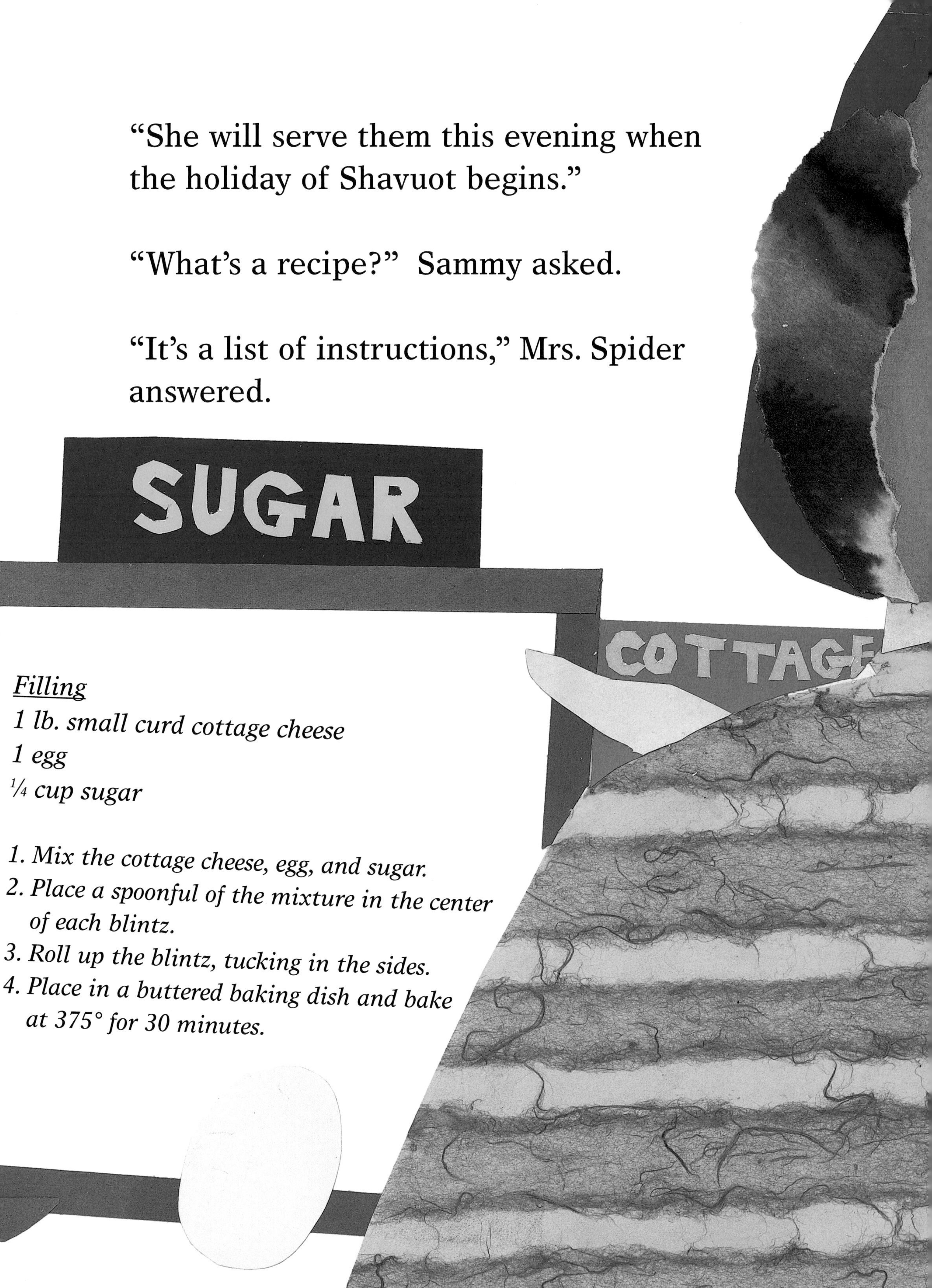

<u>Filling</u>
1 lb. small curd cottage cheese
1 egg
¼ cup sugar

1. *Mix the cottage cheese, egg, and sugar.*
2. *Place a spoonful of the mixture in the center of each blintz.*
3. *Roll up the blintz, tucking in the sides.*
4. *Place in a buttered baking dish and bake at 375° for 30 minutes.*

“FIRST
she measured
the flour.

“THEN
she added
eggs.

"NOW
she is mixing
in some milk."

“What is Mrs. Shapiro doing now?” Sammy asked.

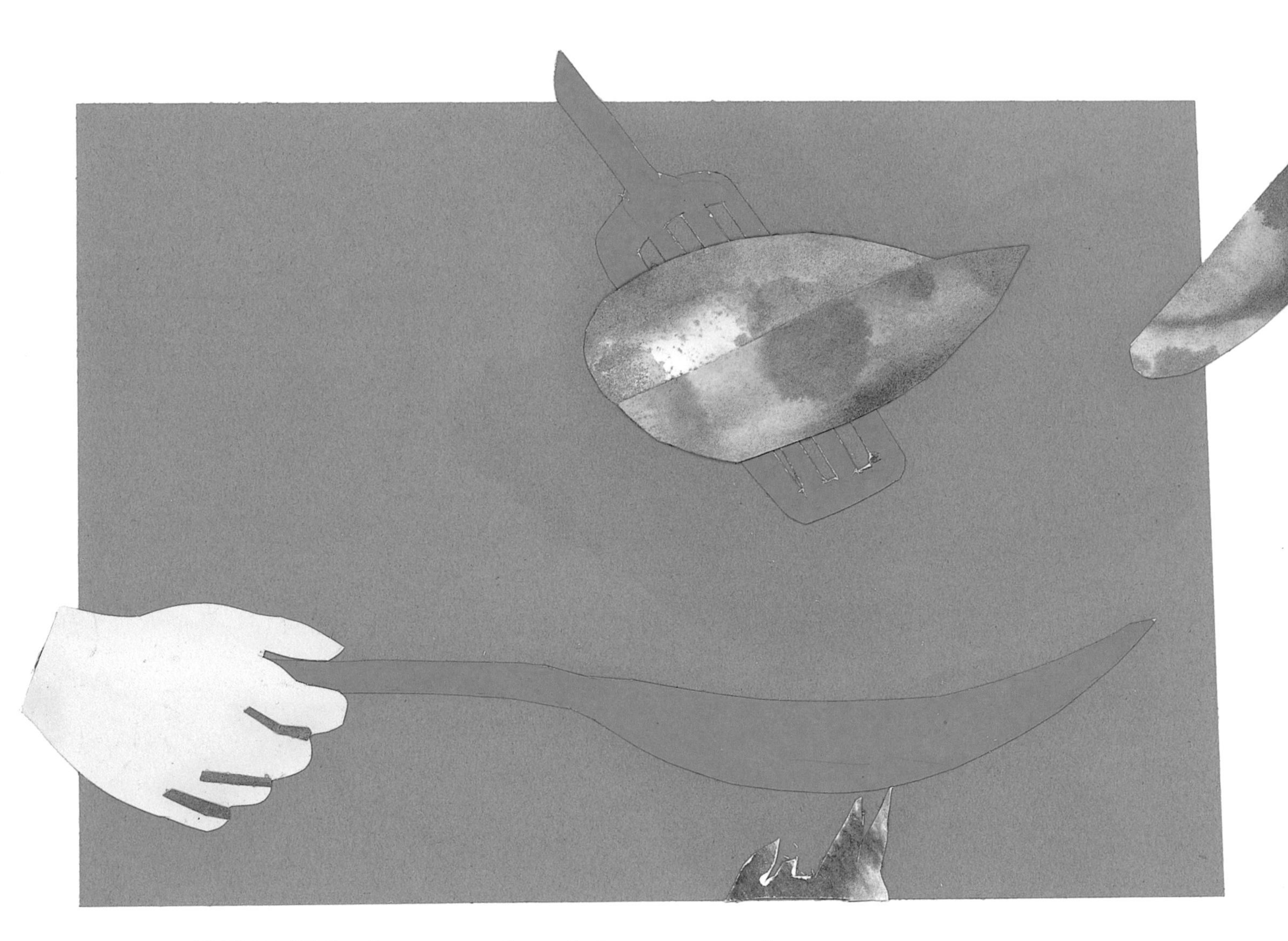

“FIRST she made thin pancakes.

“THEN she put a spoonful of cheese filling into the middle of each one.

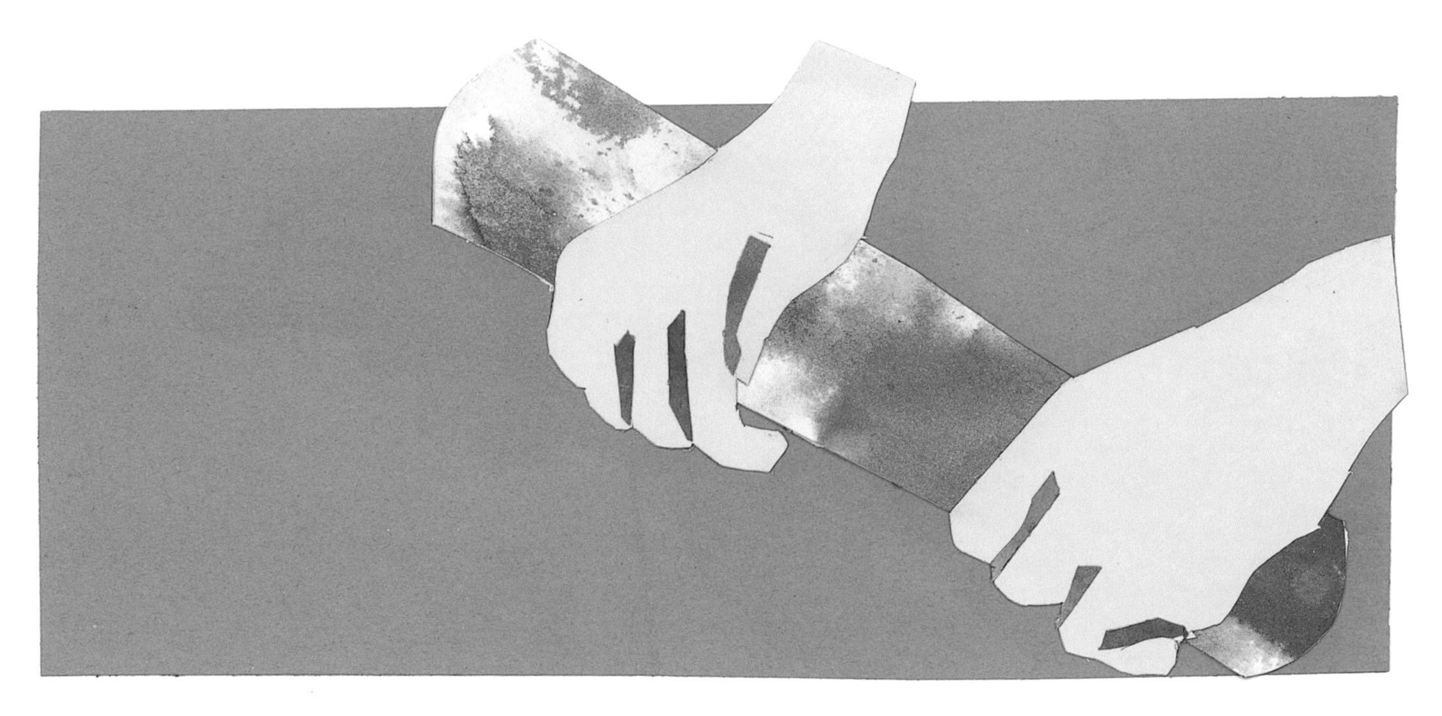

“NOW she is rolling them up to make the blintzes,” responded Mrs. Spider.

"Can we make blintzes for Shavuot?" pleaded Sammy.

"Silly little Sammy. Spiders don't celebrate Shavuot. Spiders spin webs," replied his mother.

Sammy lowered himself on a strand of webbing. He watched Mrs. Shapiro ladle some mixture into a frying pan.

Suddenly, a drop of hot oil splattered upward and barely missed Sammy, who scurried back up to his web.

"Phew! That was close," sighed Mrs. Spider.

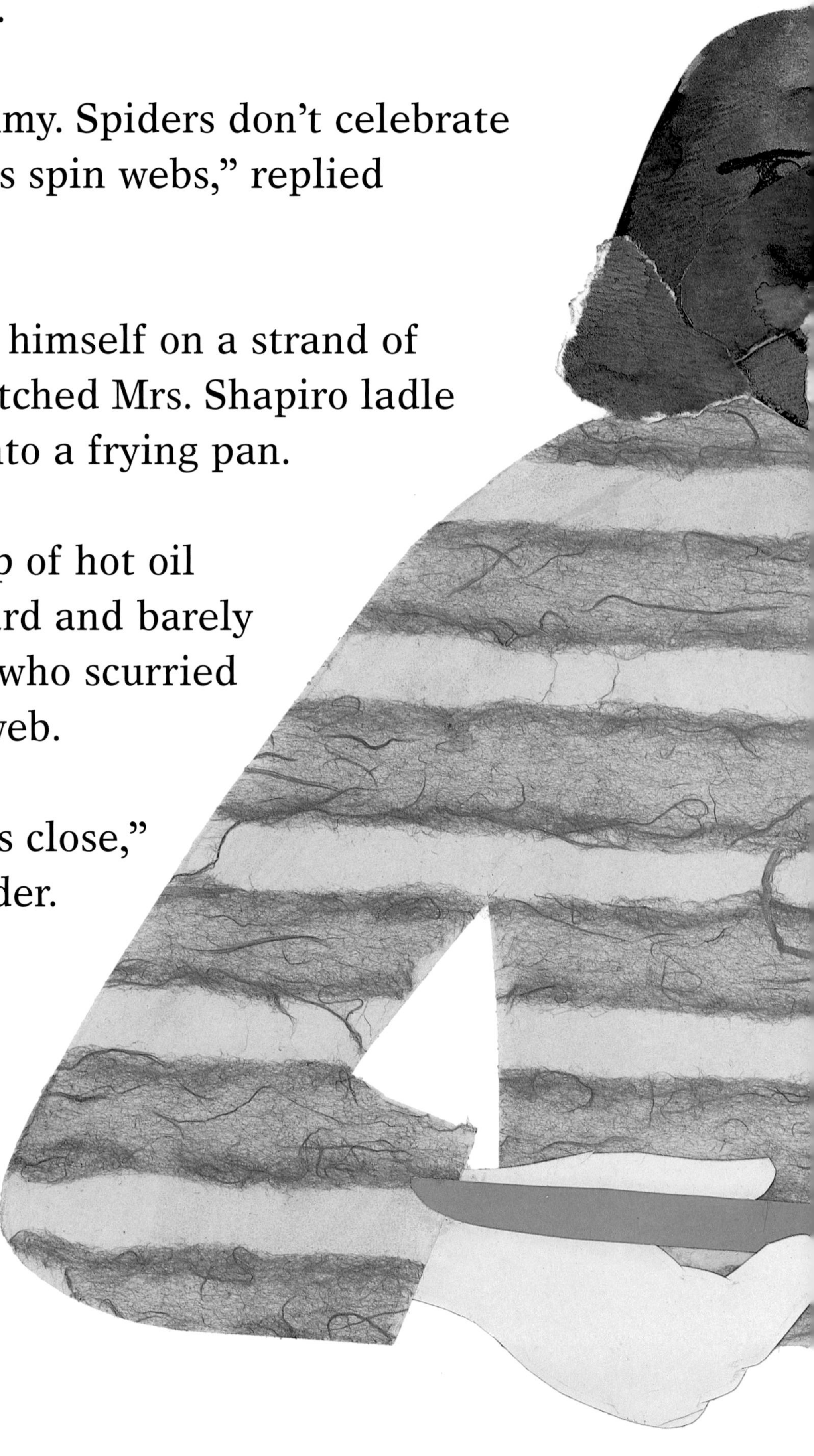

Sammy looked down
and saw Mr. Shapiro
at the sink.

"What is Mr. Shapiro doing?"
he asked his mother.

"FIRST
he washed
the berries,"
she said.

“THEN he sliced them.

“NOW he is mixing them with sugar.”

“Shavuot celebrates the first fruits of spring,” explained Mrs. Spider. “Mr. Shapiro is preparing strawberry topping for the blintzes.”

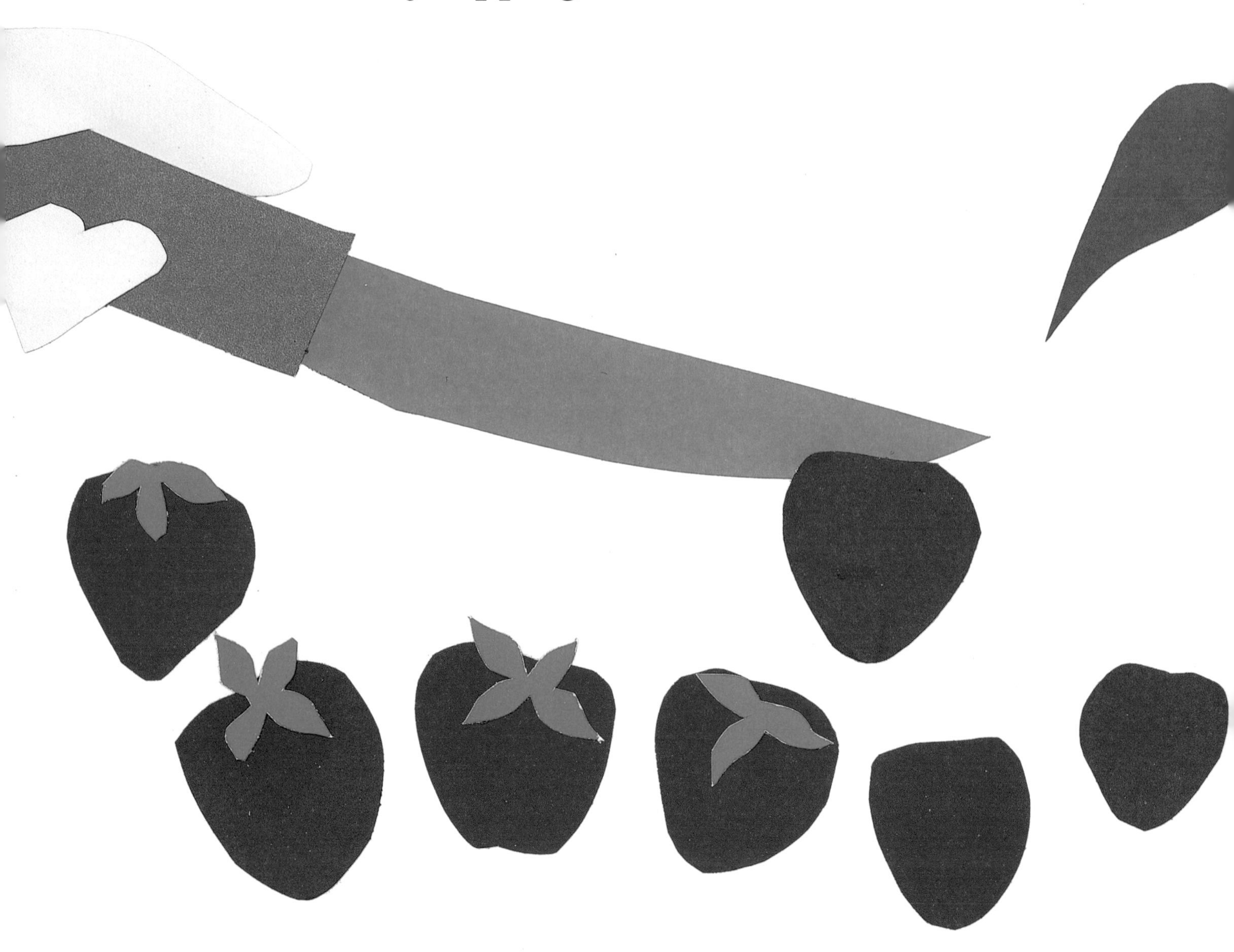

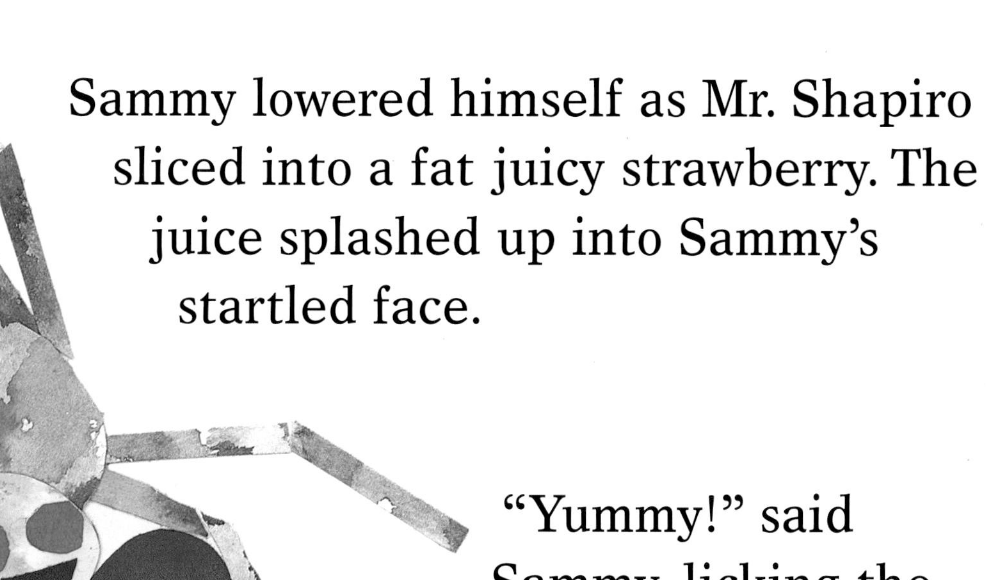

Sammy lowered himself as Mr. Shapiro sliced into a fat juicy strawberry. The juice splashed up into Sammy's startled face.

"Yummy!" said Sammy, licking the sweet juice. He climbed back toward his mother. "Would you like a taste?" he offered.

"Silly little Sammy," grinned Mrs. Spider. "Spiders don't eat strawberries. Spiders spin webs."

Just then, Josh burst into the kitchen carrying a small object.

"Is that a blintz?" asked Sammy.

"No," laughed Mrs. Spider. "It's a little Torah scroll Josh got at Hebrew school.

"It's like the large Torah scrolls that are read in synagogue on Shabbat and the holidays.

“Shavuot celebrates the time when God gave the Torah to Moses,” Mrs. Spider explained.

“FIRST Moses taught it to the Jewish people.

“THEN they taught it to their children.

"NOW it continues. Josh is learning Torah from his parents the way they learned it from theirs."

"What is it about?" asked Sammy.

“The Torah tells the story of the Jewish people. It also has rules about how to treat others with love, kindness, and respect,” said Mrs. Spider.

“Is it a recipe for living?” questioned Sammy thoughtfully.

“That’s a good way to describe it,” agreed Mrs. Spider.

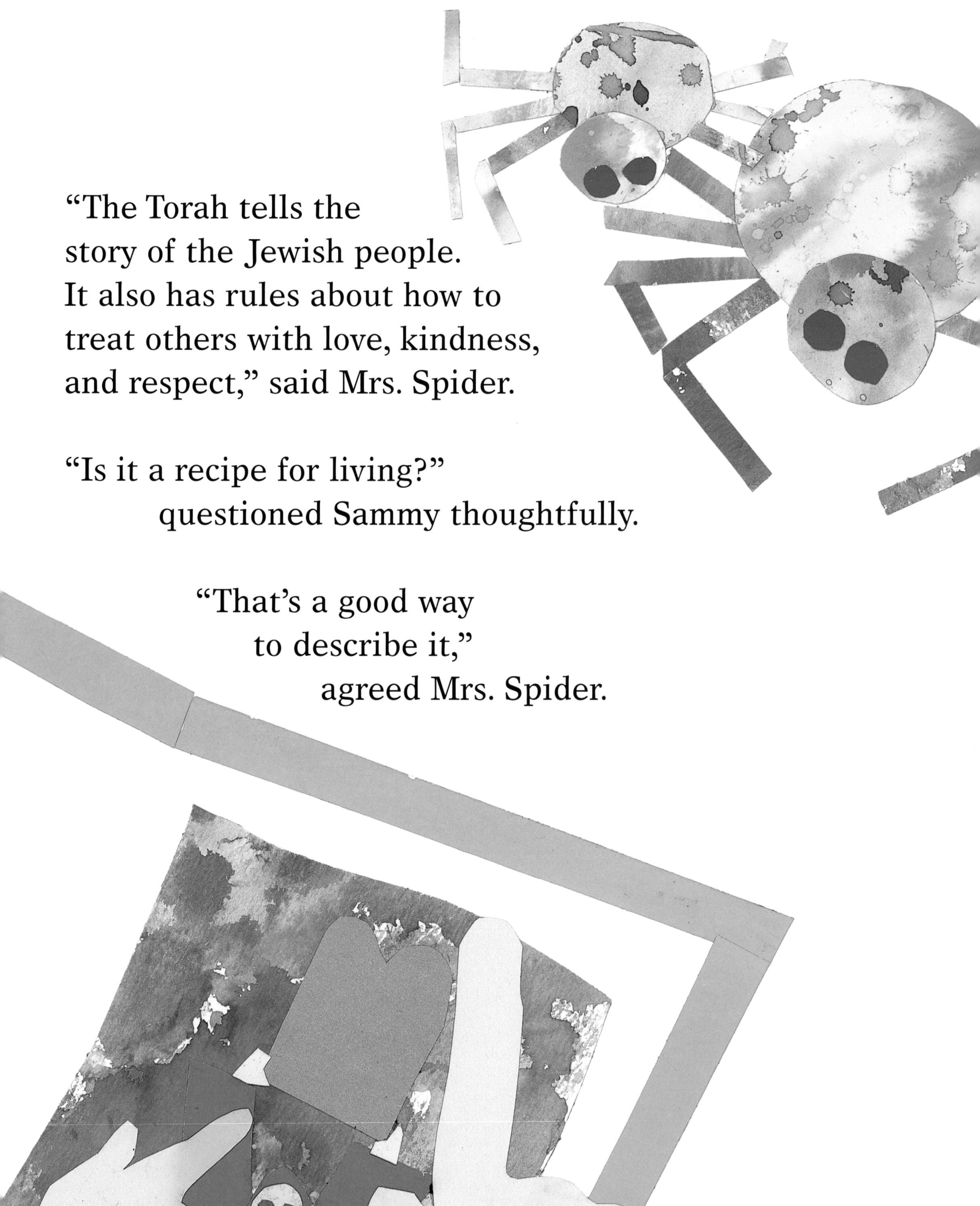

Josh gently placed the little scroll on the table next to a vase filled with fresh flowers.

"The blintzes smell delicious!" he said. "May I try one?"

"FIRST
I want you to take a
plate of blintzes to
our new neighbors,"
his mother said.

"THEN come back,
wash your hands, and
you may have
a blintz."

Eager to get a closer look at the little Torah, Sammy zoomed down and landed right in the middle of the flowers. “Achoo!” he sneezed. A fine yellow powder covered him from head to feet. Startled, he darted back to his web.

Mrs. Spider chuckled as she dusted the yellow powder off of her sneezing little Sammy. "You've had quite a day!

"FIRST you were nearly
splattered with oil,

"THEN you got
splashed with
strawberry juice,

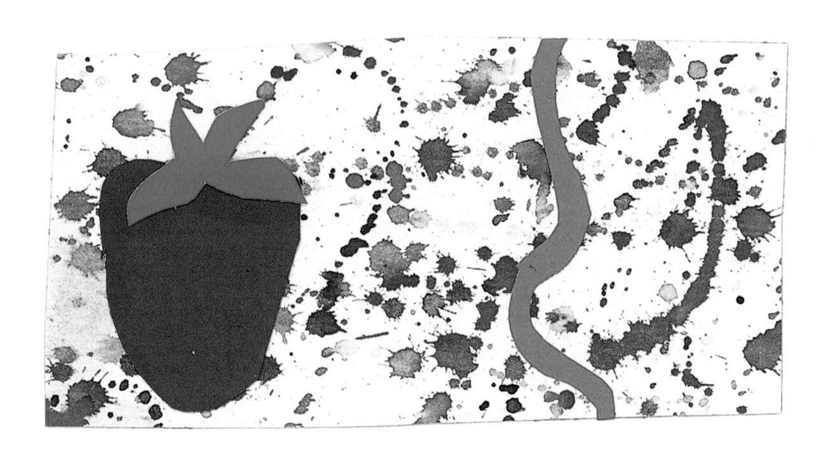

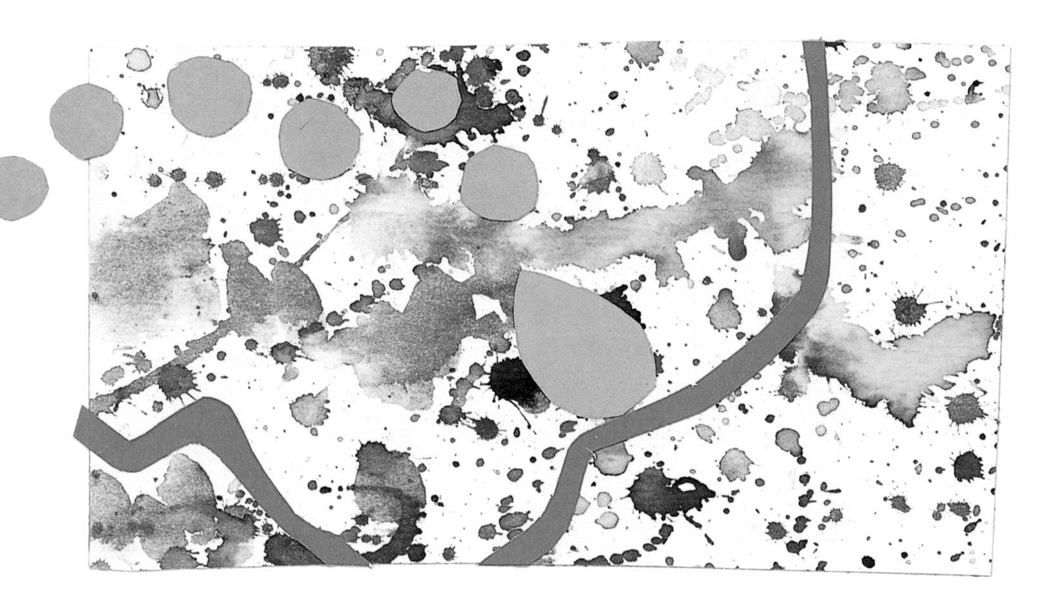

"NOW you are covered in pollen.
You must be tired."

"Mother, I think I know a spider's recipe for living," he said, yawning.

"FIRST let's get you ready for bed," said Mrs. Spider.

"THEN you can tell me what you've learned."

Mrs. Spider tucked Sammy into his web.
He whispered something in her ear.

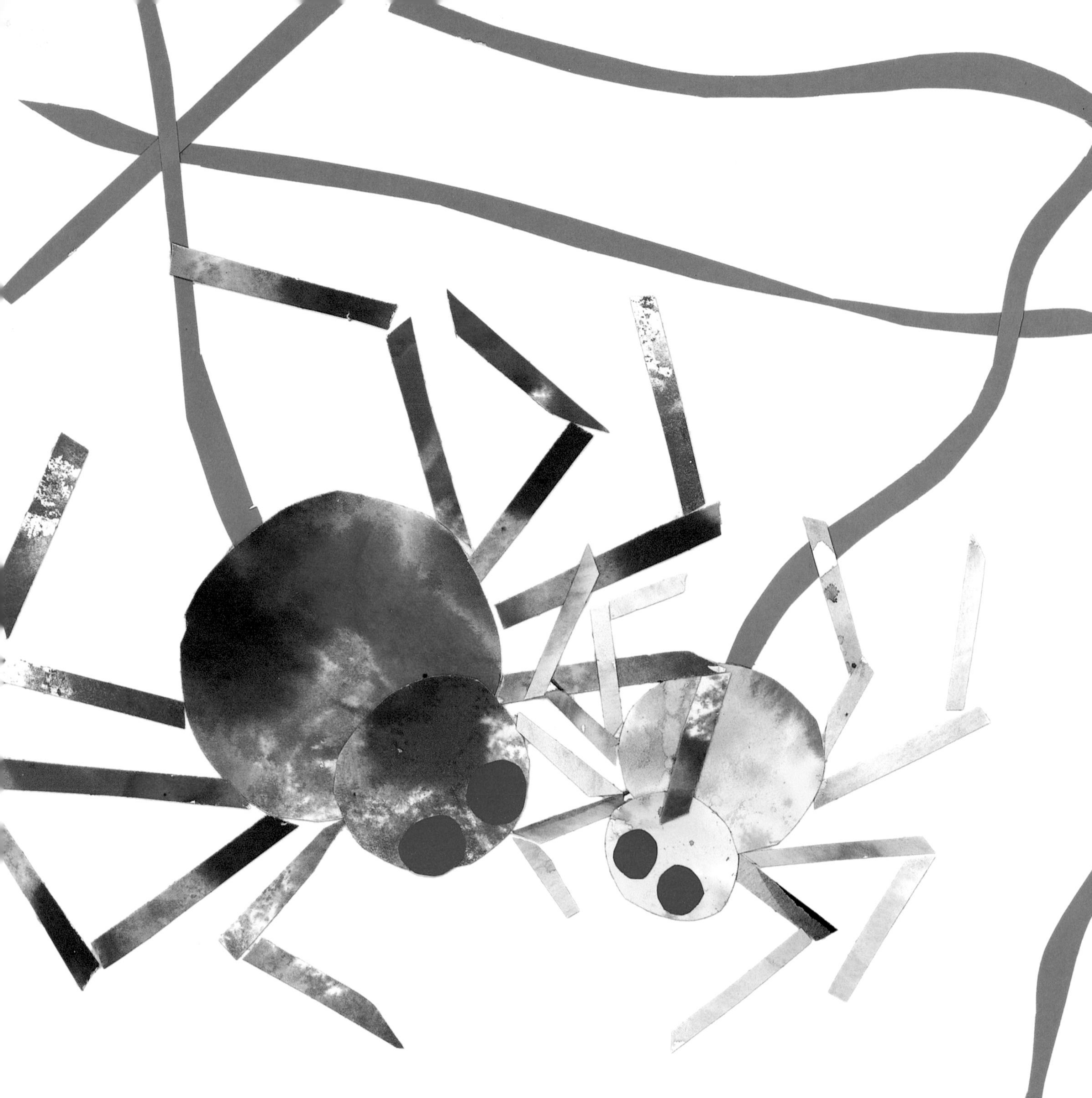

“You’re right, little Sammy,” Mrs. Spider said.
“NOW let’s say it together!”

“SPIDERS SPIN WEBS!”

Mrs. Shapiro's Blintz Recipe

Pancakes

1 cup flour

2 eggs

½ cup milk

1. *Mix the flour, eggs, and milk together. Pour a small amount of oil in a frying pan and heat.*
2. *Drop a spoonful of batter into the pan, tilting it to coat the pan.*
3. *When the blintz is lightly browned, remove it from the pan.*

Filling

1 lb. small curd cottage cheese

1 egg

¼ cup sugar

1. *Mix the cottage cheese, egg, and sugar.*
2. *Place a spoonful of the mixture in the center of each blintz.*
3. *Roll up the blintz, tucking in the sides.*
4. *Place in a buttered baking dish and bake at 375° for 30 minutes.*

About Shavuot

Shavuot means “weeks,” and the holiday is called the Feast of Weeks because it comes seven weeks after Passover. It celebrates the time that the Jewish people received the Torah on Mt. Sinai. Shavuot also marks the harvest of the first fruits of summer. It is said that the words of Torah are as sweet as milk and honey, so it is traditional to eat dairy foods, such as blintzes, at festive meals.